Sand Rips

of 8 to 10 feet

at low Water

When to the Eastward of
Sandy Point to bear N. E.
and Steer E. by S. or E.
deepest water of the Cha.
Sankoty Head bears S.
Course from North to E. S.
Dangers.

Sandy Point

Galls Rock
11 feet

Clay covered with Sand

Coskaty Bluff

A Swell when the
Wind is at N. W.

Squam Bluff

To Sail into Nantucket
Harbor: and carry the best water over
the bar on which is 9 feet, bring the Light house
to bear S. S. E. then run for it giving Brant Point
a birth and Haul in. The Buoy on the East
Flat is seen in day time.

clonuuck Island

Eall Pond

Ell Point

Capum Pond

Clift Head

9 Feet

Coatu Point

Matekit Harbour

Long Pond

Brand Point
Light House

Nantucket
Harbour

Post House

Rope Walks

NANTUCKET

N A N T U C K E T   I S L A N D

Smooth Hummock Pond

Micomit Point

Low Beach

POLLK R.

Tom Never's Bluff

Ack! The Nantucket Duckling

NANDUCKET

Published by Nanducket Books

For my numero uno, Kevin, and to
William, Harrison, and Sloane, who are loved beyond words,
often silly geese, and always my favorite ducklings.

Published by Nanducket Books
244 Madison Avenue
Suite 7888
New York, NY 10016
www.nanducket.com

Library of Congress Control Number: 2020903825
ISBN: 978-1-7340101-0-7 / eBook ISBN: 978-1-7340101-1-4
Printed in China

Inside cover map: Des Barres, Joseph F. W. Chart of Nantucket Island and the eastern half of Martha's Vineyard, 1776.

Thanks to Kevin Spurway, Jacquline East, Beth Kendall, Dan Hannon, Charles and Mary Hannon, Hugh and Rosemary Spurway, John Novielli, Keller Irons, Daniel and Emily Mazzola, Richard and Carter Bendall, David Kammerdeiner, Sam Severn, Chris Thomas, Josh Jarvis, Hope Schaefer, Kelly Bateson, Jessie Croizer, Rachel Amaral, Mia Peeled, Eddie Cruz, Debbie Thomas, Kelly Ford, Alicia Hinojosa, Brenda Hinojosa, Carol Kowlojeski, Tracy Canty, Maysoon Abed, Karen McGirk, Dan Miller, Michael Oberschneider, Susan Dunaway Thielke, Katie Thielke Groupe, The Auburn School, Ginger Andrews, and the Maria Mitchell Association.

And special thanks to Paul McCarthy for feeding the ducks!

In memory of my best friend and biggest supporter, Angela Hannon. Mom, this is that book you always told me to write!

Ack! The Nantucket Duckling

by
A.K. Spurway

illustrated by
Jacqueline East

On the island of Nantucket lived a little duckling with a big problem.

His name was Ack, and just like all the other ducklings, he could march in line behind his mother, paddle across the pond, and duck dive all afternoon. But there was one thing that made Ack different, and it was stuck right in the middle of his face.

Long and narrow with a wide brim at the end, Ack's beak was shaped more like a shiny brass trumpet than a duck bill. Worst of all, it made a funny *ack, ack, ack* sound instead of a proper *quack, quack, quack.*

All the other ducks on Goose Pond laughed at Ack because of his different sound. They covered their ears when he tried to quack, and they pulled his feathers to get him to stop. They told him his beak looked silly and strange. They even made Ack swim at the back of the duckling line.

3

One afternoon, Ack hid behind the old cherry tree beside the pond.
When he was sure nobody could see him, he cried. "I hate my beak," Ack
said to himself. "If I was just like everyone else, I'd be so much happier."

Just then, Ack heard someone approaching. Peeking around the tree, he saw
Wilson Wigglesworth, a small, shy boy who sometimes liked to feed the
ducks. Wilson always made sure that every duckling got a treat, even Ack.

But today, Wilson looked upset. Behind his large, thick glasses, Ack could see
that Wilson's eyes were red and watery. Had he been crying too?

Ack waddled closer and watched as Wilson pulled the thick glasses from his face and frowned at them. He almost looked ready to toss them into a nearby trash can, but then Wilson changed his mind and put them back on. He seemed sad. A moment later he trudged away towards his home.

As spring drew on, the days grew warmer, the flowers bloomed, and the island prepared itself for its annual Daffodil Festival. And as everyone on Nantucket knew, the very best part of the Daffodil Festival was the Duckling Parade.

Over on Goose Pond, the mother ducks
preened and polished their little ones for the
parade. And they made sure that each and
every duckling looked perfectly plumed.

9

They also warned their little ones about careless Mrs. Crabapple, who rode her bike too fast and didn't pay attention to where she was going.

She always ignored the duck crossing sign nearby, and frightened the ducks as she whizzed past the pond at break-neck speed. They would honk and quack in anger, but Mrs. Crabapple didn't seem to care.

11

As the day of the parade drew near, the young ducklings were filled with excitement and anticipation. All except Ack.

He was certain that the people watching were sure to point and laugh at him. Ack knew he had to do something.

He covered his beak with a
hat, but then he couldn't see.

He hid his beak with a
sock, but the sock was
too big.

14

He disguised his beak with a crab,
but it pinched him.

OUCH!

16

Nothing seemed to work. Ack was so frustrated! "I just can't do it," he said to his mother. "I have a useless, embarrassing beak. What's the point?"

His mother looked surprised and she took Ack under her wing. "Ack, it's true that your beak has a different shape, but it gives you a strong distinctive quack, and that's a wonderful gift for a young duck," she said.

Finally the day of the Duckling Parade arrived. Ack's mother led her brood to Orange Street, where an excited crowd had gathered to watch as the young ducks made their crossing. It seemed the whole town was there to get a glimpse of the famous duckling parade.

As the ducks families proudly began to cross, Ack hesitated and hid behind a nearby fire hydrant.

20

But there was no escape.

A friendly man noticed that Ack was all by himself. "Hey," he
shouted, "this little duckling is lost!"

Dozens of eyes turned towards Ack. His mother raced over and
collected him, quacking
her disapproval. Now
Ack had no choice.

He had to join the parade.

As he took his place in the line of ducklings, Ack looked up at the crowd that was gathering. He noticed his friend Wilson Wigglesworth was there.

Wilson's glasses were gone, and he was blinking and rubbing his eyes, as if he couldn't see much at all.

Ack watched as Wilson stepped off the curb onto the street, hoping to get a better look at the parade.

It seemed like everyone on the island was there to watch ducklings – except for Mrs. Crabapple. She was riding her bike, rushing her prize daffodils to the annual Flower Competition, dreaming of winning the coveted Dazzling Daffy award for the year's best blooms.

She was so excited that she didn't realize she was careening down the road – straight towards Wilson Wigglesworth!

25

Ack's eyes darted between Wilson and the bike.

Leaping lizards! She was about to crash straight into the boy!

26

Without thinking, Ack drew in a giant breath, opened his beak as wide as possible, and sounded the alarm.

"Ack!" he trumpeted. "ACK! ACK! ACK!" The crowd quickly turned to see what was the matter, only to gasp in horror at the accident about to unfold. But Wilson only blinked at the road, confused.

With all his might, Ack flapped his tiny wings and "ACK! ACK!! ACK!!!"-ed even louder.

The cry was so piercing it snapped Mrs. Crabapple out of her daffodil daydream. Looking up, her eyes went wide, her knuckles turned white, and the bike started skidding as she yanked on her brakes.

SCREEEEEEEEECH!

Her basket of prize daffodils went flying through the air. A woman screamed. Time stopped. Yellow petals rained down onto the crowd.

Ack flapped his wings and hopped to get a better view, expecting to see his friend crumpled on the ground. Instead, Wilson stood just inches from the bike, still blinking in surprise.

"This little duckling's a hero!" someone shouted. "His extraordinary quack saved the day!"

31

Wilson's mother ran to her son. "Wilson, why aren't you wearing your glasses?"

Wilson's cheeks went bright red as he glanced at the other children in the crowd. But then suddenly his back straightened, and his chin lifted. "I never liked my glasses, Mom," he said, "But I need them to see. And now I realize it doesn't matter so much what the other kids think."

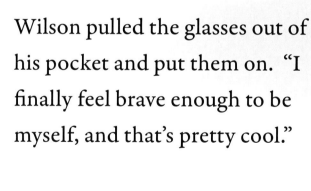

Wilson pulled the glasses out of his pocket and put them on. "I finally feel brave enough to be myself, and that's pretty cool."

Ack looked away from the boy, only to discover half the town staring right at him. But they weren't laughing at him – they were smiling and clapping!

As Ack took in their beaming faces, he noticed that some were tall, others were short. Some were darker, others lighter. Nobody talked, walked, or dressed the same. Duck or person, each was wonderfully different.

Ack's fellow ducklings shuffled him to the front to lead the Duckling Parade. The mayor arrived and led the crowd in a cheer, "Hooray for Ack! The greatest duckling in Nantucket!!"

For the first time in his life, Ack wasn't ashamed of his trumpet-shaped beak and the special sound it made. He held his head high.

Ack's mother hugged him and said, "I'm so proud of you, Ack. You're brave and special, but most important, you're not afraid to be yourself. **Always remember, you are loved just as you are.**"

Turns out that being different made Ack the luckiest duck of all!

The Real Story of the Nantucket Duckling Parade

The real story of the Nantucket ducklings began with Paul McCarthy, a Nantucket native and master woodcarver. Mr. McCarthy lived on the island and had his workshop on Orange Street, close by a tidal marsh, fed by freshwater springs, which was home to a large duck population. The ducks would march across the street to visit Mr. McCarthy, who welcomed them into his yard and fed them. At times, hundreds of ducks would visit Mr. McCarthy. The part of the street where the ducks crossed was marked with a sign – "Duck Crossing" – and it became an island landmark. Over 25 years, Mr. McCarthy got to know each and every beak – Scruffy, Clammy, Alice, Ralph, Likes to Walk, Peg Leg, and many more. Today, while Mr. McCarthy has moved off island, the sign remains. And if you're lucky enough to be there at the right time, you might even see the annual Duckling Parade.

About A.K. Spurway

A.K. Spurway has a secret...

Would you like to know what it is? Some believe it's a bit peculiar, others think it's fun. It's a talent that's hard to believe, but she learned it when she was just a child.

Spurway can speak to ducks. Quack!

And guess what? They have a lot to say. Especially her buddy Ack, the tiny duckling with a big, brave story to tell about the power of being different. It's a tale Spurway knows well. In 2004, she was diagnosed with a condition that changed her appearance and the movement of her facial expressions. Adjusting to a new normal wasn't easy, but it hasn't stopped her from doing the things she cares about most. Volunteering with the Red Cross in the aftermath of the Sri Lankan tsunami and Hurricane Katrina, Spurway learned that life can change in an instant, and every day is a gift.

This is her first book and it's dedicated to celebrating everything that's special about each of us. When Spurway isn't hanging out with her feathered friends, chasing after her three kids, or spending time with her husband, she's working on an idea Ack gave her – a clothing line that's about being daring, different, and yourself.

HA'S VIL...

OLD TOWN

CAPE POO...

MATAKIE'S BAY

Retrinty Point

Weique Beach

Wasque Point

Hause Shoals

Muskeget Island

N.E. Point

Gravel Id

Smiths Point

Muskeget Passage

To Sail through this Passage in the deepest Water bring Cape Poge to bear N.¼ W and Steer for it.

To avoid these Shoals keep Cape Poge bearing to
Southward of West until you approach the South Point of the
Horse Shoe which is steep too. The bearings of Tuckanu...
Island, as you draw near it will direct you. When Cape Po...
Bears West and Tuckanuck Island South, you are in 5 f...
And when you have Brought the Saddle of the Island to bear S...
You may Steer S.S.E. for Nantucket Harbor, or make l...
Stretches either to the Northward or Southward, the Sound l...
clear of Shoals.